Fair play

Hachette UK's policy is to use papers that are natural, renewable and recyclable products and made from wood grown in well-managed forests and other controlled sources. The logging and manufacturing processes are expected to conform to the environmental regulations of the country of origin.

Orders: please contact Bookpoint Ltd, 130 Park Drive, Milton Park, Abingdon, Oxon OX14 4SE. Telephone: +44 (0)1235 827827. Fax: +44 (0)1235 400401.
Email education@bookpoint.co.uk
Lines are open from 9 a.m. to 5 p.m., Monday to Saturday, with a 24-hour message answering service.

You can also order through our website:
www.hoddereducation.com

ISBN: 9781510481664

© Quirky Kid 2020

First published in 2016 as The Best of Friends ™ © Quirky Kid

Concept by Dr Kimberley O'Brien

Illustrations by Connah Brecon © Quirky Kid 2020

Story by Barbara Gonzalez © Quirky Kid 2020

Art direction by Leonardo Rocker

Graphic design by Lisa Diebold

This edition designed and typeset by Gary Kilpatrick

Printed in India

This edition published in 2020 by
Hodder Education,
An Hachette UK Company
Carmelite House
50 Victoria Embankment
London EC4Y 0DZ
www.hoddereducation.com

Impression number   10 9 8 7 6 5 4 3 2 1

Year   2024 2023 2022 2021 2020

A catalogue record for this title is available from the British Library.

MIX
Paper from
responsible sources
FSC™ C104740

Fair play

Activities by
Dr Kimberley O'Brien

Story by
Barbara Gonzalez

Illustrated by
Connah Brecon

Welcome to PYP Friends!

Meet the four friends who live on Quirky Lane and follow the stories of how they resolve conflict and strengthen their friendships in the school playground and local neighbourhood.

Salma

Coco

Lochie

Rafi

QUIRKY LANE

It seemed like any other day at school, but it wasn't. There was a buzz of excitement in the air and, as he stared at the clock, Lochie had one thing on his mind.

Who would be the champions?

Today was the semifinal of the greatest handball tournament they had ever played: Lochie and Rafi vs Hannah and Tim.

The competition was fierce but if they could beat Hannah and Tim, then they would make it into the grand final. Lochie was **nervous** and excited and he was just wiping his sweaty palms when …

BRRINGG!!!

The lunch bell, at last!

3

Lochie sprung out of his chair and sprinted out of the classroom to the handball court. Rafi was already there, and everyone was waiting for the game to start.

"Who do you think is going to win?" someone asked.

"Definitely Rafi and Lochie," said some of them.

"No way, Hannah and Tim are really much better players," said others.

All the kids had their opinions and cheered and clapped throughout the game every time their favourite player scored a point.

But there was one voice among the spectators that wasn't so keen.

As he watched quietly with his friends, Jake rolled his eyes at the whole business.

"This is so boring. Come on, let's go," Jake said to his friends, expecting them to follow. But they were watching the tournament and didn't hear him over all the cheering.

"Hey!" yelled Jake, "let's go!" Jake's friends heard him this time and slowly turned to follow. "I think Lochie's probably going to win it," remarked one of them. "Who cares who wins, it's just a stupid handball game!" barked Jake.

Jake's friends looked at each other and wondered why he was so angry.

Ding, Ding, Ding!
Time was up!

The game was over and Lochie and Rafi had won! The crowd roared with applause and the boys high fived each other.

Lochie was **grinning** from ear to ear. He grinned all afternoon in the classroom, and all the way home. He grinned all through dinner and even while he brushed his teeth before bed.

That night, Lochie dreamt about handball.

7

T he very next day ...

tick ...

tick ...

tick ...

L ochie had never watched anything so slow in his life. Sometimes he thought the clock wasn't moving at all!

BRRINGG!

At last!

Lochie raced out to the playground, picking up Rafi on the way. The grand final day was here and the two boys were ready to face their opponents! As they rushed to the handball court, all their supporters followed closely behind.

But ...

... something was very,

very wrong.

As Lochie and Rafi approached the handball court, they saw Jake and his friends were well into their own handball game. Lochie looked over at Rafi and wondered what to do. But Rafi was already storming over to Jake.

"Hey! This is our court! We've been playing here all week!" raged Rafi. Jake ignored him and kept playing. "Hey! Get off the court! It's ours!" repeated Rafi. Jake continued to ignore him and by now, a crowd had gathered round to see what was going on.

Lochie watched as Rafi huffed and puffed. Finally, Rafi had had enough, he charged into the handball court and took the ball from Jake just as he was about to hit it.

"Give it back!"

yelled Jake. "No! You give us our handball court back!"

The two boys were head to head and it looked like Rafi was about to hit Jake. Lochie didn't want anyone to get into trouble with the teachers, so he stepped in.

"Rafi, don't worry about it, just leave him."

But then Rafi did something unexpected.

He turned on Lochie and shoved him hard, so that Lochie almost fell to the ground.

"Hey!" cried Lochie. "What did you do that for?" Rafi was like an unstoppable bull.

"Don't tell me what to do!"

… and with that he shoved past Lochie again and disappeared into the playground. Lochie was **gobsmacked**. He was annoyed at Jake too, but couldn't understand why Rafi was taking it out on **him?**

That night, Lochie wasn't grinning at all.

"Lochie, did you win the hamball game?" asked his little sister.

"It's **hand**ball,

not **ham**ball!"

… snapped Lochie.

"Lochie, don't talk to your sister like that! She was only asking."

"Sorry Mum, sorry Meg." Lochie felt bad for **snapping at** his little sister, but he felt worse about what had happened that day.

He just couldn't stop thinking about it. In fact, he thought about it all weekend.

Maybe he could tell a teacher about it on Monday to see what they would say. Or maybe he could talk to Jake privately and explain things? And what about Rafi? Why was Rafi mad at him and what could he do to fix it?

Lochie felt awful as these questions swirled around in his head,

over and over again,

all weekend.

E arly on Monday, as the kids on Quirky Lane walked to school, Lochie felt a **knot in his belly** as they approached Rafi's house. He didn't know if Rafi was still going to be mad at him.

"Hey," said Rafi.
"Hey," replied Lochie.
"Did you bring the ball?" asked Rafi and then Lochie thought he caught a **cheeky spark** in his eyes. "Yep," he answered.
"Awesome!" said Rafi,

giving Lochie

a friendly nudge.

"By the way, sorry about the other day," he said.
Lochie smiled and was so relieved that Rafi wasn't angry at him anymore.

"That's okay. Do you still want to play the tournament together?"
"For sure!" replied Rafi. "I've been thinking about it all weekend!"
"Me too," said Lochie. "I've got this idea for how we can get the handball court back from Jake and finish the tournament ..."

"Me too!" cried Rafi,

"What's your idea?"

As they walked to school, the two friends shared their ideas and discovered that they had the same one!

"Snap!" they said and laughed together. Now it was just a matter of trying to convince Jake.

Just before the bell for lunch, Lochie and Rafi were once again watching the clock closely.

BRRINGG!

At last!

They bounded out of the classroom and straight out to the playground. They had to get to the handball court, and fast!

But when they got there, they were surprised to see that Jake and his friends had already arrived and were setting up their game. A crowd had even gathered around to watch them.

"What are you two doing here? This is our tournament and you're not in it." barked Jake.

Rafi and Lochie knew they had to stay calm for their plan to work.

"That's okay, Jake," said Lochie. "Yeah, no worries," added Rafi. "We just came over 'cause we wanted to tell you our idea."

"Not interested,"

said Jake, turning his back to Rafi and Lochie.

"Come on Jake," said Lochie. "Hear us out. We think you guys are really good at handball and we've got this idea …" But Jake interrupted: "So is that why you left us out of your tournament?"

Rafi looked at Lochie and then Lochie looked at Rafi. So that's why Jake had been so angry about the tournament!

19

They had left him out!

Rafi and Lochie realized that they probably owed Jake an apology.

Rafi looked shyly at Jake. He wasn't used to saying sorry – especially twice in one day!
"Sorry Jake," he finally said.
"Yeah, sorry Jake," added Lochie.
"It really sucks being left out."

"Well, I suppose that's okay. So, what's your big idea all about?" Jake was suddenly very interested.

So Lochie explained that if they joined their tournaments together they could have the best, the biggest, the most **mammoth**, handball tournament the playground had ever seen!

"So what do you think?" asked Lochie.

Jake wasn't convinced. "But we've already started our tournament ..." he said. "... and we've almost finished ours," replied Lochie. "But who cares, when we could have the most mammoth tournament ever?"

"Well ..." thought Jake.

"Okay. Let's do it!"

And suddenly a great cheer erupted from the crowd. "YAAAY!"

"Yay!" cried Lochie and Rafi as they gave each other a high five for their brilliant idea.

"Hey everyone, get ready for the most mammoth tournament ever!" cried Rafi to the crowd.

"Yay! Mammoth, mammoth, mammoth ...!" chanted the crowd.

That night as Lochie lay in his room thinking back on the day, he once again grinned from ear to ear. He was really pleased that everything had worked out between them and Jake, and that now there was going to be another tournament, bigger and better than the last. In fact, it was going to be mammoth.

As his eyelids grew heavy and he felt himself drifting off to sleep, he heard the chanting of all the children that day, "Mammoth, mammoth" ... and he had to smile to himself.

Yes, it was going to be mammoth indeed.

Role Play:

How to join a group

J oining a group can be challenging for anyone. However, there are lots of things we can do to make it easier. Practice makes perfect, and each time you try joining a group it gets easier. So let's practise joining a group by completing the role play that follows!

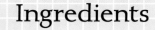

Ingredients

INITIATIVE
You may need to make the first move when it comes to joining a group.

CONFIDENCE
Trust that you will succeed. Try your best to make a good first impression.

PERSISTENCE
Finding the right group may be a case of trial and error. Never give up!

FLEXIBILITY
It's important to be flexible when you are part of a group. Take turns and try new things.

RESILIENCE
Joining groups can be complicated! If you're not made to feel welcome – bounce back and try again with another group.

Method

Step 1

Choose one person to be alone while all the others form different groups.

Step 2

The person who is alone watches the group/s and decides to join in.

Step 3

Work on your conversation starters:

What could you say to:

A very large group of kids playing handball together?

....

....

A small group of kids talking quietly on a bench?

....

....

Three of your classmates arriving together at school?

....

....

Step 4

Choose someone in the group you could talk to. Decide if you should say something or play alongside them.

Step 5

Take a step and start a conversation, or simply join in the fun.

Step 6

If you feel comfortable, keep playing along. If not, **try another group**.

Let's practise!

Read the following scenarios and write a few sentences or talk about how you would join each group. Remember you can keep looking back at the ingredients and steps on the previous pages.

The friends that you usually play with at lunchtime have gone on a bus to play sport. You see a large group of children from your class playing a chasing game on the oval.

What steps would you take before approaching the group?

....

....

What would you say or do after you join the group?

....

....

Practise this scenario with your group.

You just started at a new school. There are a lot of groups playing together at recess but you don't know anyone. Three girls your age are talking together on the bench.

What steps would you take before approaching the group?

....

What would you say or do after you join the group?

....

Practise this scenario with your group.

You recognize three kids from your school one Saturday morning at the market. You've never played with them before, and since you are walking alone, it might be nice to join them.

What steps would you take before approaching the group?

....

What would you stay or do after you join the group?

....

Practise this scenario with your group.

Glossary

Nervous (page 2)
A feeling of worry or agitation.

Grinning (page 6)
Someone that is displaying a large smile.

Gobsmacked (page 13)
To be or feel very surprised or shocked at something or someone.

Snapping at someone (page 14)
To lose control of your feelings and show anger towards someone without warning.

Knot in his belly (page 17)
A feeling of worry or concern that can be felt in your body around your tummy. Sometimes this can feel like a tummy pain, or feeling of heaviness and/or discomfort.

Cheeky spark (page 17)
A feeling of happiness and fun, which can feel a little mischievous in nature.

Mammoth (page 21)
Something huge, large or really important.